ZACKARY
RAFFLES

ZACKARY RAFFLES

by Dennis Kyte

Doubleday

New York   London   Toronto   Sydney   Auckland

For Zanderflox Flutterduck

Published by Doubleday, a division of
Bantam Doubleday Dell Publishing Group, Inc.
666 Fifth Avenue, New York, New York 10103

Doubleday and the portrayal of an anchor
with a dolphin are trademarks of
Doubleday, a division of Bantam Doubleday Dell
Publishing Group, Inc.

Library of Congress Cataloging-in-Publication Data
Kyte, Dennis
    Zackary Raffles / by Dennis Kyte.—1st ed.
p. cm.
    Summary: When the moon illuminates all the objects that frighten a
young mouse in the night, he finally conquers his terrible fear of
the dark and is able to realize the greatest wish of his sixth
birthday.
    ISBN 0-385-24652-8   ISBN 0-385-24653-6 (lib. bdg.)
    [1. Mice—Fiction.   2. Fear—Fiction.   3. Night—Fiction.
4. Birthdays—Fiction.]   I. Title.
PZ7.K993Zac 1989
[E]—dc 19   88-28238
CIP
AC
Rev.
RL:2.9
Copyright © 1989 by Dennis Kyte

Designed by: Diane Stevenson/SNAP•HAUS GRAPHICS

t the edge of Mrs. Fletcher's farm, between the barn and the creek, at the base of an old oak tree, in a patch of grass banked by wild violets, sat a little wooden house.

**I**nside the house, lying in a bed as big as your hand, under three blankets and a quilt, was Zackary Raffles. "Oh, Moon Beans!" he said. "I wish morning would hurry up and get here."

Zackary Raffles was a mouse whose sixth birthday was two days away. When a mouse was six, he could join the Mouse Soldiers, brave and true. Mouse Soldiers stand guard all day and night, protecting the other mice.

A Mouse Soldier was brave.
A Mouse Solder was true.
A Mouse Soldier was *not* afraid of the dark.
Zackary Raffles was brave . . . sort of.
Zackary Raffles was true . . . sort of.
Zackary Raffles *was* afraid of the dark.

Zackary Raffles was so afraid of the dark that he had to take a nap during the day because he almost never slept at night. The night was dark and scary. The night was full of strange noises and funny smells.

Z ackary Raffles was so afraid of the dark that he carried a lighted lantern with him, even in the day, because sometimes the sun went behind a cloud and it would get dark.

All the other mice knew that Zackary Raffles was afraid

of the dark. Some of the mice felt sorry for him. Some of the mice made fun of him. But most of the mice agreed that Zackary Raffles would never be a Mouse Soldier, brave and true.

M orning arrived and Zackary Raffles was exhausted from not sleeping again. But he dressed with special care and headed for the Mouse Soldiers' Guardhouse. When Zackary Raffles arrived, he stopped and read the words over the door. MOUSE SOLDIERS, BRAVE AND TRUE. Zackary Raffles sighed a little sigh and rang the guardhouse bell. It was breakfast time and all the Mouse Soldiers were there. One soldier opened the

door. Gathering all his courage, Zackary Raffles said, "Good morning, *squeak* sir *squeak*! Tomorrow is my sixth *squeak* birthday and I have come to *squeak* join the Mouse *squeak* Soldiers."

"In that case, you must see the Captain."

"The Captain?" Zackary Raffles gulped.

"Just follow me," the soldier said.

e led Zackary Raffles through the dining hall and out the back door to a small thatched cottage. The soldier knocked gently, opened the door, and sent Zackary Raffles inside. There were books and wonderful objects everywhere. In the corner, by the fireplace, stood an older mouse writing in a book. Without turning around, the Captain said, "So, you want to be a Mouse Soldier?"

"Yes, sir," squeaked Zackary Raffles, "how did you know?"

"I know everything," the Captain laughed. "Sit down, my boy." The Captain finished his writing, then walked over to Zackary Raffles. "Do you think you can pass the Three Tests of Courage to become a Mouse Soldier, brave and true?"

Zackary Raffles tried not to stare at the floor as he nervously answered, "I *squeak* hope so."

fter breakfast the Mouse Soldiers took Zack-
ary Raffles out behind the cow barn to where
the pigs lived. There, they stretched some
twine across the pig slop. On the other side of the trough,
the big mean cat PERCY slept in the sun. Zackary Raffles
gulped. The Captain said, "You must walk the Rope of Courage
and return. If you are not PERCY's breakfast and do not fall
down into the pig slop, you will pass the first test."

ackary Raffles carefully climbed to the top of the fence. He looked across and he looked down. He looked at the sleeping heap of cat fur that was PERCY. Was PERCY asleep or just pretending? Zackary Raffles muttered, "Oh, Moon Beans!," took a deep breath, and put one pointed paw on the rope. The rope swayed and trembled. The other side looked so far away. Zackary Raffles said to himself, "If I just take it one step at a time, I think I can do it."

He took a second step and looked down. *"Whoa!"* he cried
as he almost stumbled. "If I don't look down and I put my
arms out for balance, I won't fall," he thought. One step at a
time, with his arms out for balance, he finally reached the
other side. PERCY had not awakened. Zackary Raffles turned
and quickly walked back. When he returned, the soldiers
cheered and then the Captain gave him his Mouse Soldier
cape, his first reward for bravery.

ood," said the Captain. "Now you must solve the Mysterious Riddle: 'What is lighter than the wind?'" Confused, Zackary Raffles wandered off to begin his search for the answer.

First, he went into the barn and looked around. "Something that is lighter than the wind must be something small," Zackary Raffles said to himself. "So"—he went on—"I know what it isn't. It isn't the cow or the sheep or the shovel or the milk can or the ladder or the hen or her eggs." Zackary Raffles climbed up and up and up to the rafters of the barn and onto the roof. He tiptoed along the top of the roof to the weathervane. There, in a starling's nest, he found the answer. "A feather is lighter than the wind," Zackary Raffles said excitedly to himself and climbed back down to where the Mouse Soldiers were waiting.

"Bravo!" said the Captain as he took the feather, placed it in a magnificent hat, and presented it to Zackary Raffles as his second reward.

"nly one more test, my little friend," the Captain said. "You must spend the night standing guard on Lookout Rock."

Zackary Raffles's knees began to tremble. "Maybe I could walk the Rope of Courage again, instead?"

"No," said the Captain sternly. "You must stand guard and prove that you are not afraid of the dark. Then you will receive your sword and will finally become a Mouse Soldier, brave and true."

"But I *am* afraid!" thought Zackary Raffles. Suddenly, his mind was filled with all the scary, creepy things that make up the dark. "Oh, Moon Beans!" whimpered Zackary Raffles as the soldiers escorted him up to the gatehouse on Lookout Rock. From there he could almost see the entire farm. He could see the entire vegetable garden, which at night was the deepest, darkest, and scariest place of all.

arkness was falling as the soldiers began their return march. The Captain looked back and called, "Be brave! We shall return for you in the morning."

The sun had almost disappeared as Zackary Raffles climbed into the gatehouse on Lookout Rock. "Rustle . . . rustle . . . crack!"

"What was that?" Zackary Raffles said aloud, hearing something in the garden. He wiggled his whiskers. "There's that funny smell too." Suddenly something big and black swooped down from overhead. *"Eeow!!"* he cried. "That's it . . . I am going home."

e ran through the rows of corn. He ran through the rows of lettuce. He ran through the rows of tomatoes, peas, and beans. He ran so fast that only when he could run no farther and stopped to catch his breath did he realize that he had lost his Mouse Soldier hat and cape.

"Oh no!" cried Zackary Raffles. "I worked so hard for my hat and cape!" And, without thinking, Zackary Raffles turned around and ran back into the darkest parts of the garden. He searched and searched until he found them.

"Oh, Moon Beans!" Zackary exclaimed, clutching his hat and cape. "I was afraid I had lost them." Suddenly Zackary Raffles froze. Then his face screwed up in confusion. And then his whole body relaxed and he sat down to think. "Hmm . . . look at me. I'm not trembling. I don't feel afraid. I walked the Rope of Courage. I solved the Mysterious Riddle and I did it all by myself. And now I have spent almost the whole night in the garden in the dark. I realize there is really nothing for me to fear." Zackary Raffles put on his hat and cape. He picked up his lantern and marched back to Lookout Rock. Once there, he looked out into the darkness, held up his lantern, and said, "I won't be needing this anymore." With a deep breath, Zackary Raffles blew out the candle.

he new day dawned—beautiful and cloudless. When the Captain and his soldiers arrived, they found Zackary Raffles still standing at attention on top of Lookout Rock.

"Good morning," the Captain called. The Mouse Soldiers lined up behind the Captain as Zackary Raffles climbed down to join them. After digging around in his duffel bag, the Captain pulled out a gleaming new sword.

Zackary Raffles stuttered, "But . . . b-but . . . how did you know I would be here? I might have run home . . . I might

have been afraid of the dark . . . or something." They all laughed.

"Because, Zackary Raffles," the Captain said, "we could all see from the other two tests that you were brave and true and that you wouldn't be afraid of the dark. You didn't have to prove it to us . . . you just had to prove it to yourself."

Zackary Raffles was so proud. He knelt down on one knee and the Captain presented him with the sword of the Mouse Soldier.

Soon friends and villagers arrived, singing and carrying a splendid birthday cake. The mice began to sing "Happy Birthday!" Someone

said, "Blow out your candles and make a wish!"
He took a deep breath and blew out all his
candles and smiled because he had already made
his wish come true.

Zackary
Raffles
was a mouse soldier,
brave and true.